© 1994, Editorial LIBSA
  Published by GRANGE BOOKS,
  an imprint of Grange Books plc
  The Grange, Grange Yard
  London SE1 3AG

Published 1994

Illustrated by: JULIAN JORDAN and EVA LOPEZ

Text by: María de Calonje
Translated by: Carmen Healy
Phototypesetting by: Versal Composición, S.L.
Printed by: Gráficas Reunidas, S.A.

ISBN: 1-85627-618-X Legal Dep.: M 19.103 - 1994

Aladdin and his Magic Lamp

Aladdin was the son of a poor tailor named Mustafah who lived in a rich city of the Orient. Mustafah died when Aladdin was very small and his mother had to spin cotton night and day to support herself and her son.

Because she worked so much, she was tired and had little time to worry about bringing up her son.

Aladdin grew up in the streets without ever learning a trade with which he could earn money to help her.

On a summer day, while Aladdin played with his friends in the market, an old man approached him and asked, "Are you not Aladdin, the son of the tailor Mustafah?"

"Yes, sir," answered the boy, "but my father died a long time ago."

Hearing these words, the old man, who was really an African magician, threw his arms around Aladdin's neck. Crying, he exclaimed, "I am your Uncle Salim. Your father was my brother. Take me to your house, I want to meet your mother."

The lad accompanied his so-called uncle to meet his mother.

"I would have liked to offer you a meal, but we are very poor and have nothing," the woman said.

"Do not worry, take these coins and buy whatever you need. I am a rich merchant and I want to help you."

While they had supper, the so-called uncle said, "I can see that you are very poor, but I suppose Aladdin has learned a trade by now."

Aladdin lowered his head in shame. His poor mother answered for him, "He hasn't learned anything, he just roams the streets playing with his friends."

"That is not right. I thought perhaps that you could come with me to India. You will learn many things and later I can help you to start a shop so that you can sell fine cloth."

Aladdin and his mother accepted delightedly.

The next day, Aladdin set off with his uncle on a splendid camel. They travelled until nightfall. They camped in a narrow valley, overshadowed by a huge mountain.

"Go and fetch wood to make a good fire, I have to tell you a secret," said the magician.

Aladdin had soon gathered a pile of firewood. The magician set it on fire and, when the flames grew, he threw in powder from a strange flask. At the same time he pronounced some magic words in a language that Aladdin didn't understand.

In that instant the earth opened and there appeared a great stone slab with an iron ring.

Aladdin was so frighted that he wanted to run away, but the magician calmed him saying, "If you obey me nothing will happen to you and you won't regret it. Underneath that stone there is a hidden treasure that will make us richer than all the kings in the world. But you must do exactly as I say. Take the ring and lift the slab."

The boy did just as his uncle said. With all his strength he lifted the stone and, before his amazed eyes, there appeared a stairway leading down to a deep cave.

"Go down the stairway, through a corridor that will take you to a lovely garden with tree. filled with marvellous fruit. At the end of the garden you will find a wall with a niche and in it you will see a lamp. Empty the oil out of it, then bring it to me."

Aladdin reached the lamp, but instead of oil it contained a very dirty ring that he slipped onto his finger.

As he was returning to the
entrance, he stopped in the
garden and crammed his pockets
with all the multicoloured fruits
that he could!

When he reached the foot of the staircase, Aladdin saw Salim's eyes fixed on the lamp. It was a cold, cruel and greedy stare. The boy was very frightened.

"Give me the lamp," yelled the magician impatiently.

"First help me, I can't get up with everything I have in my pockets."

"Hand me the lamp immediately or you will be destroyed," screamed the so-called uncle furiously.

"No," said Aladdin, "I know you're not my uncle and I don't have to obey you."

"Of course I'm not your uncle. I used you because only a boy whose name was Aladdin could get me the lamp."

When he realised that Aladdin took no notice of him, he became furious and threw powder on the fire again pronouncing two magic words. At once the stone slab returned to its place and closed the entrance to the cave.

For two days Aladdin remained in the dark, without food or drink. In his despair he began to wring his hands and in doing so, without realising it, rubbed the ring that he had found in the lamp.

Suddenly an enormous genie appeared who said to him, "I am the slave of the ring and I will obey your every command."

"Take me from here," ordered Aladdin. Instantly the earth opened. The genie took Aladdin in his arms and at tremendous speed took him to the door of his house.

The following day his mother found him
sleeping peacefully in his bed. When Aladdin
awoke he showed her the ring and the lamp
and told her every detail of what had
happened.

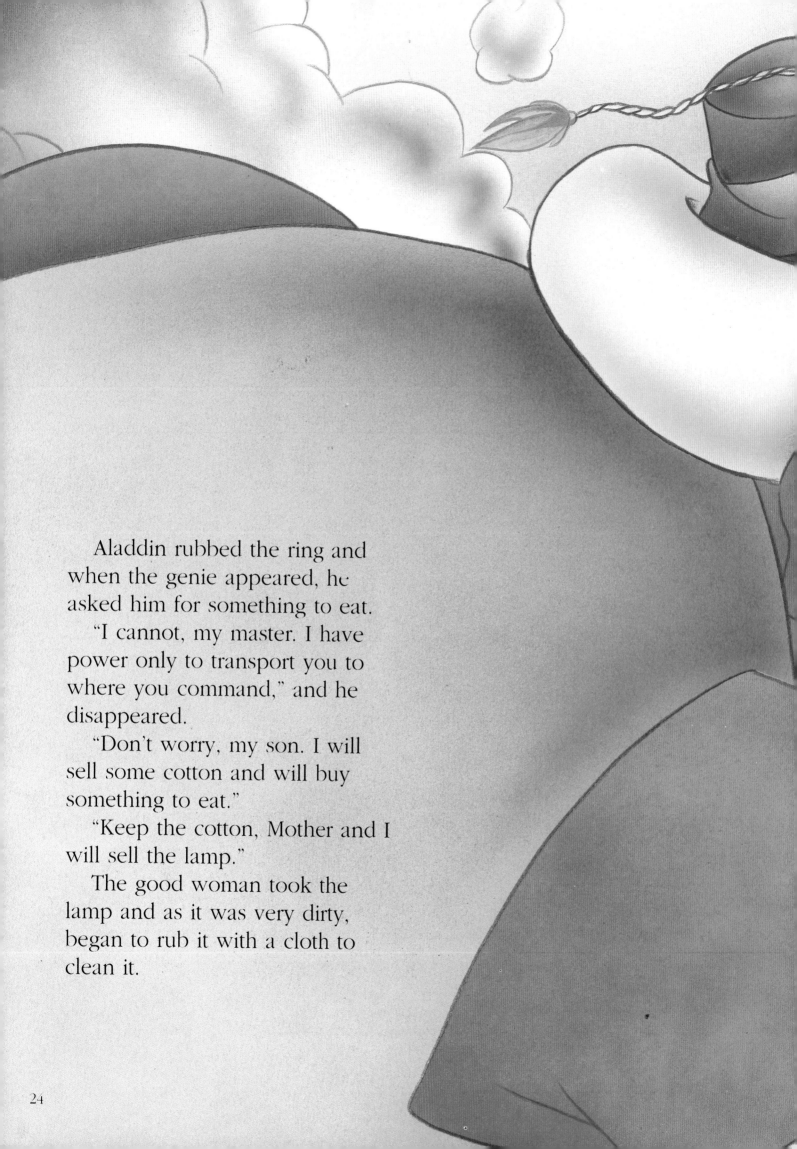

Aladdin rubbed the ring and when the genie appeared, he asked him for something to eat.

"I cannot, my master. I have power only to transport you to where you command," and he disappeared.

"Don't worry, my son. I will sell some cotton and will buy something to eat."

"Keep the cotton, Mother and I will sell the lamp."

The good woman took the lamp and as it was very dirty, began to rub it with a cloth to clean it.

Instantly a horrifying genie appeared who said with a terrible voice, "What do you wish? I am the slave of the lamp. Command and I will obey."

Aladdin took the lamp from his mother's hands and asked the genie for a good meal.

The genie disappeared. A little later he returned with a great silver tray full of exquisite foods. The command fulfilled, he went back into the lamp.

After that day, Aladdin and his mother never had have to worry about anything. The genie supplied them with everything they needed.

Aladdin began to make frequent visits to the market, intent on learning how to become a successful merchant.

He then realised that the fruits that he had taken in that marvellous garden were really precious jewels.

One day when Aladdin was walking through the city, he passed the sultan's daughter. She was accompanied by many guards and maidservants.

Her beauty was famous throughout the kingdom and beyond. Many princes and kings had asked for her hand. She had refused them all.

She was so lovely that Aladdin immediately fell in love with her.

He told his mother how he felt and begged her to ask the sultan for his daughter's hand, but she laughed and said, "My son, you must have gone mad to wish for such a thing."

Then Aladdin showed her the precious jewels that he had picked up in the mysterious garden. They decided to offer them to the sultan in the hope that such a splendid gift would please him and he would consent to their wishes.

The following day, the good woman presented herself before the sultan with her best clothes and, showing him the marvellous gems, she made known her son's request.

Before such a magnificent present, the sultan remained thoughtful trying to give a reply.

"Tell your son that I will give him my daughter's hand if, in a single day, he can build a palace worthy of her."

When the mother gave him the sultan's message, Aladdin locked himself in his room and rubbed his magic lamp. He asked the genie to build a palace of the richest marble, encrusted with precious jewels and surrounded by a garden far lovelier than the sultan's.

When on the next day the sultan saw such a splendid palace, he was very impressed and agreed to the wedding.

Only a few days later, with great rejoicing, Aladdin's wedding to the princess was celebrated. The young man knew how to win over the princess' love and happily they began a new life.

Meanwhile, back in Africa, the evil magician discovered through his magic powers that Aladdin had not died in the cave and that, thanks to the magic lamp he was very wealthy.

He was furious, and set off for the Orient intent on revenge.

When the evil magician arrived in the city, he bought some new lamps in the market and made his way to the palace calling, "Who wants to exchange new lamps for old lamps?"

The princess who was on the balcony, hearing the offer, thought of Aladdin's dirty old lamp. She did not realise its value and offered it to the old man.

The magician exchanged it for a shiny new lamp and then set off in a hurry for the forest.

At nightfall, he rubbed the lamp and, when the genie appeared, he ordered, "I command you to take me, the palace and the princess, to my domains in Africa."

The genie obediently took the palace into his powerful arms, uprooting it from the ground. Then with the magician hanging on to his neck, he flew away with Aladdin's wonderful palace leaving a big hole where it had stood.

It's impossible to imagine the terrible anger that the sultan felt when he saw that the palace and the princess had vanished. Suspecting that Aladdin was a sorcerer, he sent his soldiers to look for him intent on having him beheaded.

When Aladdin heard about what had happened, he went to see the sultan and told him the truth about his adventure.

"I am willing to spare your life," the sultan said, "if you return my daughter to me before forty days and forty nights have passed.»

In desperation, Aladdin remembered the genie of the ring and asked him to quickly take him to the place where the princess and the palace could be found.

In a flash, the genie of the ring took Aladdin to the faraway African country where the evil magician had transported his palace and his beloved kidnapped princess wife.

The princess was at that moment in the window crying bitterly. Seeing Aladdin, she was filled with joy. Scaling the walls, he reached his wife's room and there he heard all about what had happened.

"Tell me," he asked the princess, "where is the lamp now?"

"That evil man shows it to me every day to make me suffer, but it doesn't leave his side night or day."

Between the two of them they devised a plan to recover the lamp and free themselves of the evil magician forever.

The princess put on her finest clothes and invited the magician to dine with her. When they were seated at the table, she offered him a glass of wine. Flattered by such attention the magician drank the wine offered to him and was distracted for a few moments.

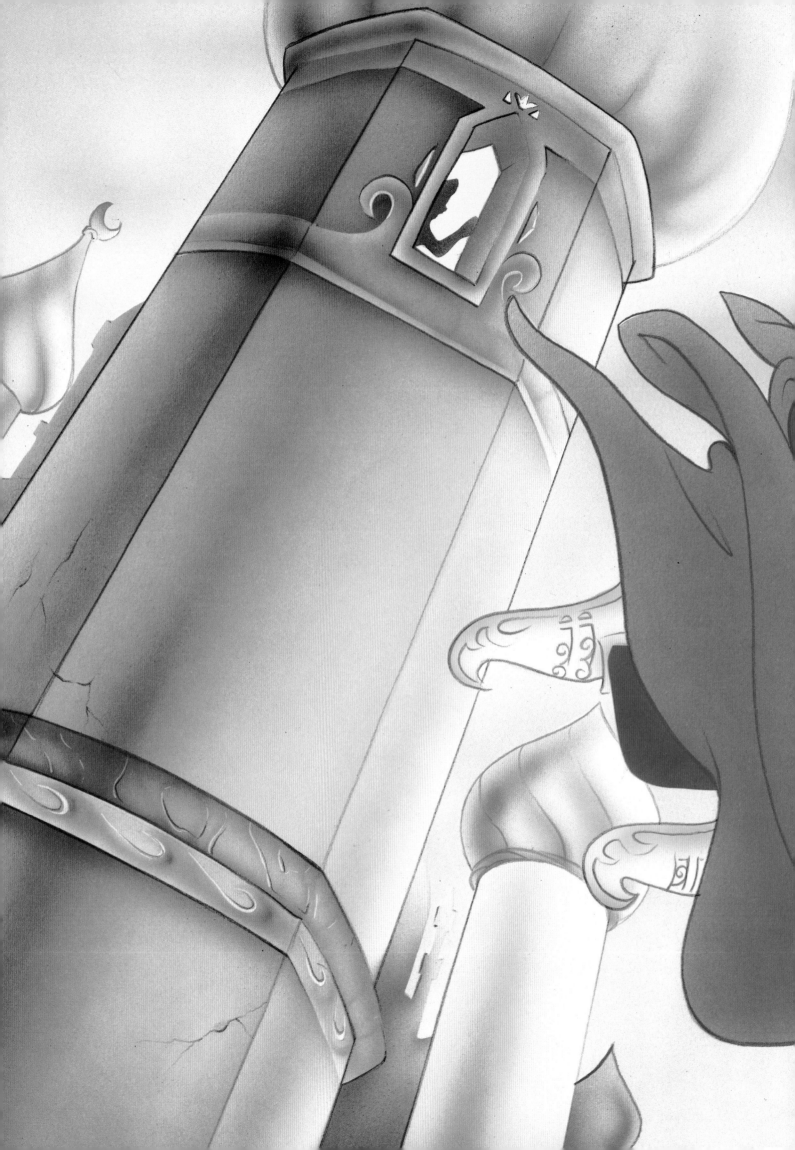

Aladdin, who was hidden behind some curtains, seized the opportunity to grab the magic lamp and then pushed the magician so hard that he fell out of the window to certain death.

He made the genie appear and ordered him to return them to the Orient along with the palace.

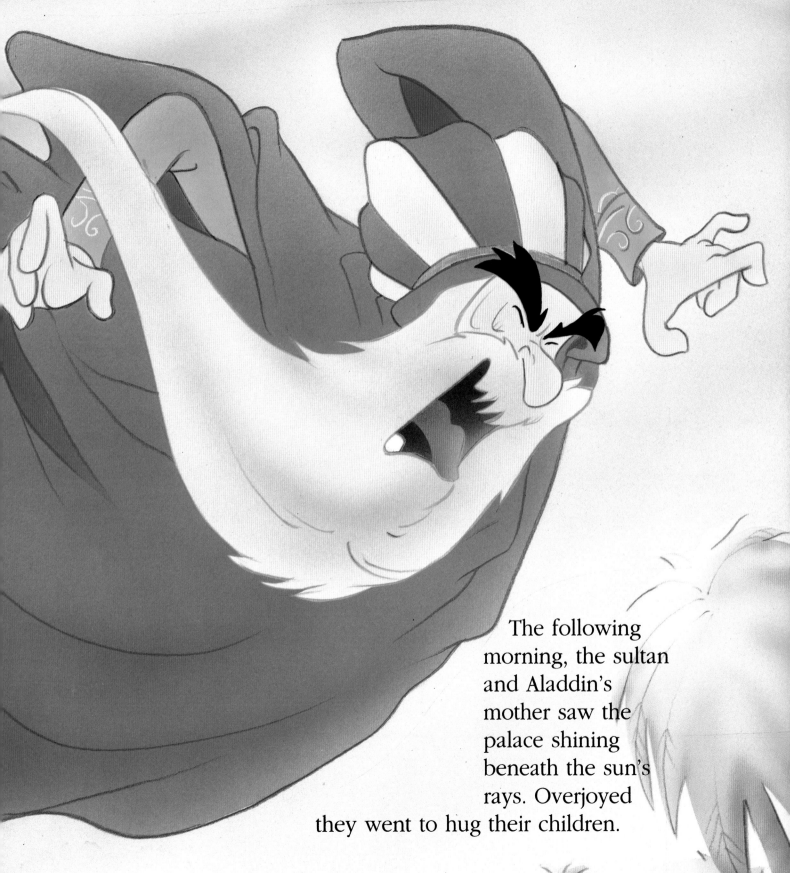

The following morning, the sultan and Aladdin's mother saw the palace shining beneath the sun's rays. Overjoyed they went to hug their children.

To celebrate their return, the sultan
ordered that festivities were to be
arranged that lasted a whole week.

Aladdin and his wife lived happily
ever after. When the sultan died,
Aladdin ascended to the throne and
reigned in the Orient for many years
loved by his people.